This

_____

A BEGINNER'S GUIDE TO
PRIVATE INVESTIGATION

HATPIN
(YOU NEVER KNOW WHEN THAT WILL COME IN HANDY)

HAT

BOW TIE

MURRAY
PIGEON/PRIVATE INVESTIGATOR

PRIVATE INVESTIGATOR : a pigeon or person whose job it is to solve crimes.

Also known as: detective, sleuth, gumshoe, private eye, P.I.

EQUIPMENT

NOTEBOOK — PENCIL
SPARE PENCIL

MAGNIFYING GLASS

DETECTING HATS

FEDORA

BERET

BOWLER

HOMBURG

CAP

BOATER

DEER STALKER

PORK PIE

CLOCHE

TORCH

BRAIN FOOD AKA SNACKS

A BAG TO CARRY EQUIPMENT AND CLUES

SNACKS

1. DELICIOUS BUT NOISY *CRUNCH!*

POPCORN

CRISPS

2. PERFECT HANDHELD SNACKS

PIE

HOTDOG

SANDWICH

3. QUIET BUT IMPRACTICAL

wibble

JELLY

TIPS

1. DON'T DRAW ATTENTION TO YOURSELF

SERIOUSLY DON'T FORGET THE SNACKS

2. QUESTION EVERYTHING

EVERYTHING!

3. PRACTISE YOUR THINKING POSE

4. BE A GOOD LISTENER

5. ASK TOUGH QUESTIONS

6. BLEND IN WITH THE LOCALS

ARE YOU READY TO SOLVE YOUR FIRST CASE?

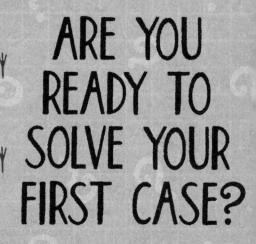

THE DAILY QUA

HAWKEYE HAMILTON

BEAKY GARRILL

The Corrections Dept.

The corrections department would like to apologise for a typographical error in yesterday's issue. Readers were led to believe that the Bird-drain Bath Company could assist with pluming problems. This is not the case. We apologise for any contusion clawed

Flaming O's CANDLE EMPORIUM

FOR MY GRANDAD
who loved detective stories,
my sister who likes them, **and my brother**
whose opinion remains a mystery.

Chloe

Jackson

Isla

Rayne

Ben

& JONNY

First published in Great Britain in 2017 by Andersen Press Ltd.
This paperback edition first published in Great Britain in 2018 by Andersen Press Ltd.,
20 VAUXHALL BRIDGE ROAD, LONDON SW1V 2SA

Copyright © Meg McLaren 2017

The right of Meg McLaren to be identified as the author and illustrator of this work has been asserted by her in accordance with the copyright, designs and patents act, 1988

1 3 5 7 9 10 8 6 4 2
PRINTED AND BOUND IN CHINA

BRITISH LIBRARY CATALOGUE IN PUBLICATION DATA AVAILABLE

ISBN 978 1 78344 598 1

CULTUR VULTUR

Your guide to this season's hottest trends

Ⓐ ANDERSEN PRESS

PIGEON P.I.

PRIVATE INVESTIGATORS

DON'T COME MORE HARDBOILED THAN THIS!

WE'LL CRACK ANY CASE

WRITTEN AND ILLUSTRATED BY

★ MEG McLAREN ★

Business was slow,
just the way I liked it.

PIGEON P.I.
TWO BEAKS ARE BETTER THAN ONE

CLOSED

Cap'n Rik's TASTY TUNA

MISSING
PET COCKATOO "CURLY"

LAST SEEN AT HOME, ADMIRING HIS OWN REFLECTION
LIKES: MIRRORS, SHINY OBJECTS, SOFT FURNISHINGS
LOVES: HIS OWNER, MRS HIGGINS-SMYTHE
DISLIKES: THE GREAT OUTDOORS
IF SIGHTED PLEASE CALL 555-2513

My partner Stanley had
skipped town a while back,
so I'd decided to
take things easy.

Then the Kid showed up.

She'd been around for a while.

It was time to find out why.

She said she'd come to the city with friends, ready for adventure, but they'd found it a little too soon...

She'd had a narrow escape but her friends hadn't been so lucky.

No one had seen them since.

I told her I didn't take cases anymore.

But she was pretty convincing.

"Come back tomorrow and we'll talk," I said. But she didn't.

I didn't see her again for weeks.
When I finally did, it was too late.

The police were busy on a big case. I was going to have to do this alone.

News travels fast
in this town, especially
the bad kind.

Word on the wire
was that birds had been
going missing all over.

All the evidence
pointed to the
Red Herring
Bar and Grill.

It was time to take
a closer look.

AND STAY OUT!

Something someone didn't want me to see.

when something caught my eye.

I was in the right place,
I just needed to find another way inside.

The Kid turned out to be a genius at picking locks.
Everything was going well until...

As usual, my curiosity got the better of me.
Everyone else made it out safely,

YOU AGAIN?

GO!

but it looked like
my wings were
clipped for good.

After all, that's what partners are for.

PLUMAGE PLUNDERER PINCHED BY PREVIOUS PARTNER, PIGEON P.I.

With another jailbird behind bars, the streets were safe again and I planned to keep them that way.

SLURP!

The EARLY BIRD

SLURP!

With a little help, of course.

ADVANCED DETECTION

MISSING
GOLDEN EGG
CALL: G. GOOSE

I've made an egg-citing discovery!

Egg-cellent work!

HAVE A WITTY LINE READY WHEN YOU SOLVE YOUR CASE

DISCUSS IDEAS WITH YOUR PARTNER

What if...?

No. But then we could...

No. How about..?

I don't think so. What if we..?

YES!

PRACTISE TAKING NOTES

TRY TO REMEMBER WHAT ORDER THINGS HAPPEN AND AT WHAT TIME

Hmm...

Vee's notes
7.30	Woke up
7.31	Got up
7.40	Ate apple for breakfast
8.00	Murray woke up
8.01	Murray reports his apple missing
8.02	THE SEARCH BEGINS!

FAMOUS DETECTIVES

LIEUTENANT COLUMBA
(COLUMBA LEGATUS)

J.B. FLEDGLING

BONJOUR!

MONSIEUR PARROT

MISS MARBLE-D WOOD QUAIL

SHERSTORK HOLMES

DUCK TRACY

BE LIGHT ON
YOUR FEET

Quack?

QUACK!

CONFIDENCE IS
THE KEY TO
EVERY DISGUISE

CARRY A BOOK OR NEWSPAPER TO HIDE BEHIND

But Monsieur Parrot is about to solve the case!

DETECTIVE EXAM

NOTEBOOKS READY?
ALL OF THE ANSWERS CAN BE FOUND IN THE STORY.

1. Name Vee's two missing friends.

2. How many yellow sprinkles are on Chief's doughnut?

3. What type of fish does Cap'n Rik catch?

4. Which bird doesn't appear on the tea towel?

COMMON GULL   BARROW SPARROW   RACING PIGEON

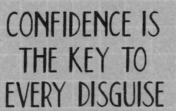

5. What is the name of Murray and Vee's detective agency?

(DON'T GET DISTRACTED)

TEST YOUR MEMORY

1. STUDY THE TRAY OF OBJECTS FOR ONE MINUTE.

2. CLOSE YOUR EYES WHILE ONE OBJECT IS REMOVED.

3. OPEN YOUR EYES—CAN YOU SPOT WHAT'S MISSING?

Did you guess what's missing?

HOW MANY DID YOU GET RIGHT?

5. Bird's Eye View

4. Barrow sparrow

3. Tuna

2. 5

1. Ruby and Jimmy

ANSWERS

MEG McLAREN

MEG McLAREN is an author, illustrator, printmaker and unapologetic whodunnit aficionado. She lives in Inverness, Scotland (where she is rebuilding her natural Scots' resolve against the cold) with her other half, Jon, and Wilson, her canine partner in crime.

Murray MacMurray

CASE NO. 621

CONFIDENTIAL

...e and clever, this ...s enquiring mind ...ought by some of ...st powers around ...e, and a little bird ...Vee too.

Vee

WILSON PICKLE

Approach with caution

CAS

CONFIDENTIAL

CASE NO. 621

Feathered friends are ... missing all over t... investigat...